I Like to Read® books, created by award-winning picture book artists as well as talented newcomers, instill confidence and the joy of reading in new readers.

We want to hear every new reader say, "I like to read!"

Visit our website for flash cards, activities, and more about the series:
www.holidayhouse.com/ILiketoRead
#ILTR
This book has been tested by an educational expert
and determined to be a guided reading level D.

For elephants and sea creatures, and
those who work to keep them safe

I LIKE TO READ is a registered trademark of Holiday House Publishing, Inc.

Copyright © 2018 by Steve Henry
All Rights Reserved
HOLIDAY HOUSE is registered in the U.S. Patent and Trademark Office.
Printed and bound in December 2017 at Tien Wah Press, Johor Bahru, Johor, Malaysia.
The artwork was created with ink, watercolor, gouache, and acrylic on 300 lb. hot press watercolor paper.
www.holidayhouse.com
First Edition
1 3 5 7 9 10 8 6 4 2

Library of Congress Cataloging-in-Publication Data is available.

ISBN 978-0-8234-3773-3 (hardcover)
ISBN 978-0-8234-3890-7 (paperback)

HIDE!

Steve Henry

I Like to Read®

HOLIDAY HOUSE • NEW YORK

Mike naps.

Pat sees a fish.

Pat sees more fish.

Pat sees more and more.

The fish have fun.

A shark!

Pat can't hide.

Pat still can't hide.

Pat needs help.

The shark has Pat.

Pat is safe.

Now Mike has fun.

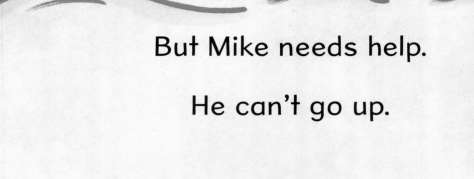

But Mike needs help.

He can't go up.

The fish help Mike.

Pat and Mike are safe.

They nap.

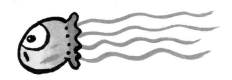

ALSO BY **Steve Henry**

HAPPY CAT

★ "This cheery entry in the I Like to Read series successfully tells a simple tale and creates a sense of community using just 20 unique words."
—*Kirkus Reviews* (starred review)

CAT GOT A LOT

"An ideal choice for a beginning reader."
—*School Library Journal*